P9-CFA-042

Please Don't Eat the Children

Don't miss the other spine-tingling

Secrets of Dripping Fang adventures!

BOOK ONE:

The Onts

BOOK TWO:

Treachery and Betrayal at Jolly Days

BOOK THREE:

The Vampire's Curse

BOOK FOUR:

Fall of the House of Mandible

BOOK FIVE:

The Shluffmuffin Boy Is History

BOOK SIX:

Attack of the Giant Octopus

SECRETS OF

DRIPPING FANG

BOOK SEVEN

Please Don't Eat the Children

DAN GREENBURG

Illustrations by SCOTT M. FISCHER

HARCOURT, INC.

Orlando Austin New York San Diego Toronto London

I want to thank my editor, Allyn Johnston, for her macabre yet soulful sense of humor, for her eagerness to explore ideas beyond the bounds of taste, for understanding an author's poignant thirst for praise, and for helping me say exactly what I'm trying to say, except more gooder.
I also want to thank Scott M. Fischer, an artist with dizzying technical abilities and a demented genius at combining terror and humor in the same illustration.
—D. G.

www.HarcourtBooks.com

Library of Congress Cataloging-in-Publication Data
Greenburg, Dan.
Secrets of Dripping Fang. Book seven, Please don't eat the children/
Dan Greenburg; [illustrations by] Scott M. Fischer.
p. cm.
Summary: While trying to convince the FBI that giant ants are kidnapping and enslaving the citizens of Cincinnati, twins Wally and Cheyenne Shluffmuffin, with the help of their vampire father, escape the clutches of the enormous ghouls who want to adopt—and eat—them.
[1. Twins—Fiction. 2. Brothers and sisters—Fiction. 3. Ants—Fiction. 4. Vampires—Fiction. 5. Cincinnati (Ohio)—Fiction.]
I. Fischer, Scott M., ill. II. Title. III. Title: Please don't eat the children. IV. Title: Please do not eat the children.
PZ7.G8278Seh 2007
[Fic]—dc22 2006026947
ISBN 978-0-15-206047-3

Text set in Meridien
Designed by Linda Lockowitz

First edition
A C E G H F D B

Printed in the United States of America

For Judith and Zack

with spooky love

—D. G.

Contents

Please Don't Eat the Children

CHAPTER 1

The Adopters Are Coming! The Adopters Are Coming!

"Cheyenne, Wally, fabulous news!" cried Hortense Jolly, owner of the Jolly Days Orphanage. "I have people in the visiting room who might be willing to adopt you. And guess what! They even live in Dripping Fang Forest, a place you already know and love!"

The Shluffmuffin twins were on their hands and knees on the kitchen floor, scrubbing mung from between the tiles with ammonia and boiling water.

"We *know* Dripping Fang Forest," said Wally, his eyes smarting from ammonia fumes, "but we don't *love* it, Miss Jolly. And we don't need anyone to adopt us. We already have a perfectly good father."

"But, darling, you *know* how the Child Welfare Bureau feels about vampire dads who can't support their children," said Hortense. "Why do you think they took you away from him and brought you back here? And why won't anybody give your father a job?"

"Employers have a stupid prejudice against the living dead," said Cheyenne. "Poor Dad. It's not *his* fault he doesn't have a pulse. He didn't *ask* to drown in a Porta Potti." She sneezed and blew her nose into a tissue.

"We can talk about all this later, children," said Hortense, shepherding them briskly out of the kitchen. "Right now I want you to get into that visiting room and charm the Stumpfs."

"What if we *hate* the Stumpfs?" asked Wally. "Will you force us to let them adopt us?"

"Of course not," said Hortense. "Not if you hate them."

"You promise?" asked Cheyenne, sneezing again. "On your word of honor?"

"I promise on my word of honor, okay?" said Hortense with a weary smile. "Now get into that visiting room and be charming."

The first thing Cheyenne and Wally noticed about the couple in the visiting room was their teeth. They were yellow and triangular, like a shark's, and extremely sharp looking. *Did their teeth grow that way naturally,* Wally wondered, *or did they file them into points?*

The second thing they noticed about the couple was how fat they were. Not pleasantly chubby like The Pillsbury Doughboy, but grossly, waddlingly obese, like hippos. It looked as though heavy bags of water had been glued to their bodies under their clothes.

"Mr. and Mrs. Stumpf," said Hortense, "may I present the Shluffmuffin twins, Cheyenne and Wally. They're excellent dishwashers, pot scrubbers, and floor waxers. They do windows, and they've had all their shots."

"Oh my," said Mrs. Stumpf, "they look lovely. But so *skinny.* What do you feed these poor things?"

Mrs. Stumpf had greasy skin, especially around her mouth, and she smelled vaguely of rancid cooking oil.

"Madam," said Hortense, "our chef, Maurice—who, I'm proud to say, was trained at the world-famous Cordon Bleu cooking school in Paris, France—prepares these orphans only the finest of gourmet meals. For example, for breakfast today he made them fluffy soufflés with

caramelized apples, hot cocoa topped with crème fraîche, and individual puff pastries with amusing little faces made out of chocolate chips, which he began preparing before the sun was even up."

Wally had to force his lips together to keep from laughing. Breakfast was the usual—stale bread crusts and gruel the color of mucus, with little green floaty things that looked like boogers. The orphanage had never had a chef, and Maurice

was the name of a mangy rat that hung around the kitchen and snatched whatever food wasn't locked up.

"I wish *we* could come here for breakfast sometime," said Mr. Stumpf dreamily. The talk of all that gourmet food was making him drool down several chins onto his shirtfront. "Tell me, have the twins ever had major surgery? We don't want to adopt kids who've had any bodily organs removed."

"Oh no, no surgery," said Hortense, looking at the twins. "Am I right, children?"

"We had our tonsils out when we were two," said Cheyenne. "It didn't hurt much, and afterward they gave us ice cream. Chocolate peanut-butter swirl, I think."

Mr. and Mrs. Stumpf exchanged a look.

"Tonsils aren't important to us, are they, Poopsie?" said Mrs. Stumpf.

"Not really, Dumpling," said Mr. Stumpf.

"As long as they're not missing any other organs," said Mrs. Stumpf. "We do like to get all the parts they came with. Heh-heh." She giggled and impulsively grabbed Cheyenne for a fast squeeze. "Oooh, these children are just *delicious,* aren't they, Wolfgang?"

"Truly delicious," said Mr. Stumpf. "I could just eat them right up." He gave Wally's arm a pinch. "You a football player, young man?"

"Not at all," said Wally.

Mr. Stumpf stank from stale cigarettes and perspiration. "When I was in the fifth grade," he said, "I played fullback. Weighed in at barely two-eighty in those days. If we fattened you up a little, I bet we could make a fullback out of you yet. Feed you fried pork chops with lots of fat, deep-fried ham hocks, grits floating in lard—that sort of thing. Like to put on fifty or sixty pounds, young fella?"

"No, sir," said Wally. "I like the way I am."

"Good boy," said Mr. Stumpf.

"Well, Mrs. Jolly," said Mrs. Stumpf, "we've seen enough. We'll take 'em—as is. Where do we sign?"

"Just make out a check for twelve hundred dollars, and I'll get the papers," said Hortense.

Cheyenne and Wally looked panicky.

"Miss Jolly, can we talk to you a moment?" Wally asked.

"Certainly, dear," said Hortense. When she left the visiting room, the twins ran after her.

"You aren't really going to make us go with those people, are you, Miss Jolly?" said Cheyenne.

"Why not?" said Hortense, rummaging through a desk in the adjoining room, looking for adoption papers. "They seem like decent people."

"We hate them," said Wally.

"Oh, you'll get used to them after a while," said Hortense. "Don't be such a baby."

"But you said you wouldn't force us to go with anybody we hated," said Cheyenne. "You *promised.* On your word of *honor.*"

"I never said that," said Hortense, finding the forms and shutting the drawer smartly.

"You did so," said Cheyenne. "Didn't she, Wally?"

"She sure did," said Wally.

"Well, I changed my mind," said Hortense. "What do you have against the Stumpfs, anyway? They look like lovely people. And they certainly seem to like the two of *you.*"

"Sure, they like us," said Wally. "They want to *eat* us. Didn't you hear what they said? 'Oooh, these children are just *delicious.*' 'I could just eat them right up.' Didn't you hear that?"

"Oh, Wally, those are just figures of speech," said Hortense. "Lots of people say those kinds of things when they think somebody's cute."

"No, Miss Jolly, they were *serious,*" said Cheyenne, sneezing and then blowing her nose. "Didn't you hear all that stuff about operations and surgery? They don't want to get cheated out of any of our body parts."

"Don't be ridiculous," said Hortense. "They just want to be sure you are healthy, just like you would if you were buying a cow."

"They want to fatten us up," said Wally. "They want to feed us fried ham hocks and lard. They want us to be fat so there'll be more of us to eat. Did you see how fat they are and what sharp teeth they have?"

"Now, now, children," said Hortense, gathering up the papers and grabbing a ballpoint pen. "We mustn't be prejudiced against people because they happen to be a little overweight."

"A *little* overweight?" said Wally. "Miss Jolly, these people aren't over*weight,* they're *hippos.* They're *whales.* They weigh more than eighteen-wheel tractor-trailers."

"*Sssshhh!* They'll hear you," warned Hortense harshly.

"Who cares?" said Cheyenne. "We don't want to be adopted by them. You can't make us!"

"Oh, can't I?" said Hortense. She laughed unpleasantly. "We'll see about that."

She strode out of the room.

"Wally, what are we going to do?" cried Cheyenne. "Can we call Dad?"

"I'll call him," said Wally. He took the phone

off Hortense's desk and dialed the number of their friends the Spydelles' house.

After four rings Shirley Spydelle answered. "Hello?" she said.

"Shirley, it's me, Wally. We're in terrible trouble!"

"Again?" asked Shirley. "What is it this time?" Shirley was Edgar Spydelle's wife, and she was terrific, better than most humans. Over the phone, you couldn't even tell she was an enormous spider.

"Some people named the Stumpfs are going to adopt us," said Wally. "They're really creepy, and we don't want to go with them, but Miss Jolly is going to make us. They live in Dripping Fang Forest. Do you know them?"

"The Stumpfs?" Shirley repeated. "*Mmm.* Oh yes, Wolfgang and Fritzi. They're . . . a little strange."

"A little strange?" said Wally. "Shirley, they're gigantic, hippo-sized *ghouls*."

"Oh my, I don't think they're ghouls, dear."

"They are," said Wally. "We can't let them

adopt us. But Hortense says we have nothing to say about it. What can we do, Shirley? Is Dad there?"

"I'll put him right on, dear. Just a minute."

Dad got on the phone. "Hi, sweetheart," he said, "what's this about being adopted by ghouls?"

"It's true, Dad," said Wally. "Hortense is letting them adopt us, even though she promised she wouldn't make us go with anybody we hate. She's in there right now, helping them fill out the adoption papers. Can you help us?"

"I'm on my way," said Dad, his voice shifting into grim. "I'll be there as fast as I can. Try and stall them."

CHAPTER 2

Hello, You Must Be Going

"Why, Mr. Shluffmuffin," said Hortense uneasily, opening the front door, "what an unexpected pleasure. What are *you* doing here?"

"I need to speak to you about a matter of some urgency," said Dad, leaning forward, trying to push his way into the house. "May I come inside?"

"Now is not the best time, I'm afraid," said Hortense, blocking the doorway with her hip. "What is this in reference to, by the way?"

"Cheyenne and Wally tell me they're about to be adopted by somebody they hate," said Dad. "I'd like to talk to you about that."

"The Stumpfs?" said Hortense, smiling. "A lovely couple. I'm afraid there's nothing to talk about. They've just signed all the papers, initialed all the clauses, and given me a check."

"Well, *I* want to adopt the twins myself," said Dad. "I am, after all, their father."

"Yes, of course you are, and that's very sweet," said Hortense, "but I'm afraid they're already sold—um, adopted. It's too late. Besides, I couldn't allow you to adopt them."

"Why not?"

"A very good reason, Mr. Shluffmuffin. If I release the twins into your custody, I would need to be paid my twelve-hundred-dollar adoption fee. And you have made it abundantly clear that you aren't willing to consider such a thing."

Dad nodded impatiently. "What if I *were* willing to pay to adopt my own children?"

"Do you have twelve hundred dollars?" asked Hortense.

"Well, I'm not sure," said Dad. "I'd have to check."

"Even if you had the money, Mr. Shluffmuffin," said Hortense archly, "I couldn't do it—I'd be in violation of the Child Welfare Bureau."

"What if I could get the twelve hundred dollars, Miss Jolly?"

"Apparently you haven't heard what I said, Mr. Shluffmuffin. I said I cannot be in violation of the Child Welf—"

"What if I could get *more* than twelve hundred dollars, Miss Jolly?" Dad asked.

"More than twelve hundred, you say?"

"Yes."

"*Mmm.* How *much* more?"

"What if I could get . . . fourteen hundred dollars?" Dad asked.

Deep in thought, Hortense Jolly extended her lips and smooshed them up to her nose. "If you could get *fifteen* hundred dollars, Mr. Shluffmuffin," she said. "Well, naturally I couldn't be in violation of the Child Welfare Bureau by releasing the children into the custody of somebody they specifically said was not a qualified adopter. However . . ."

"However," said Dad, jumping aboard her train of thought, "if an *unknown* party—not me, of course, but someone *like* me—were to come back here with fifteen hundred dollars, then perhaps . . . ?"

"If it were not you but someone *like* you," said Hortense, "then what possible reason could I have for denying that person the right to adopt these children?"

Dad looked at Hortense for a long moment. "Thank you, Miss Jolly," he said. "Somebody—I can't say who just now—will be in touch with you in a couple of days."

"I can wait twenty-four hours, Mr. Shluffmuffin," said Hortense Jolly. "Twenty-four hours *max.*" She closed the door.

"Who was that at the front door, Miss Jolly?" asked Cheyenne. "Was that our dad?"

"No, no," said Hortense. "It was somebody wanting to sell me encyclopedias."

The Stumpfs were waiting in the visiting room with expectant smiles.

"So," said Mrs. Stumpf, "may we take the twins home with us now?"

"I'm afraid not," said Hortense. "There's been

a temporary snag. But if you come back here tomorrow at the same time, I'll have them all packed up and ready to go."

"What is this snag you speak of?" said Mr. Stumpf.

"Just a technical matter," said Hortense. "Come back tomorrow at this time and the Shluffmuffin twins are yours."

"You've got our money. They'd better be ready to leave with us tomorrow," said Mr. Stumpf darkly.

CHAPTER 3

In Some Cases Your Loan Can Even Be Approved If You Have No Credit at All or If You Have Even Been Convicted of Armed Robbery

"So that's my situation," said Dad to Edgar and Shirley Spydelle. "Either I come up with fifteen hundred dollars within twenty-four hours or Cheyenne and Wally get adopted by people they hate. Is there any way you guys could lend me that kind of money?"

"My word," said Edgar in his endearing British accent. "I certainly wish we could. Unfortunately, old chap, we're rather strapped ourselves."

He tapped the ashes out of his pipe and refilled it with fragrant tobacco he kept in a zippered plastic pouch in his tweed jacket. The tobacco smelled sweet, like a combination of apples, nuts, caramel, burnt sugar, and autumn leaves, not like anything that would grow tumors in your mouth.

"I think I could scrape together about five hundred dollars," said Edgar's wife, Shirley. "Would that help?"

"Thank you, it would," said Dad. "Now, where could I get the other thousand?"

"Why not try a bank?" said Shirley.

The bank hummed with customers drawn by the scent of freshly minted money. Dad was escorted toward the back, to a desk flanked by two chairs. He sat down on one side, and a bank officer, a man with colorless hair and skin and very thin lips, sat down on the other.

"So, Mr. Shluffmuffin," said the bank officer with a plastic smile, "how might we help you today?"

The bank officer's shirt collar was buttoned too tightly, and the veins in his neck stood out as if somebody were choking him.

"I'd like to borrow a thousand dollars," said Dad.

"Excellent," said the bank officer, his smile becoming sunnier. "Lending people money is what we do best. I assume you can prove to us you'd be able to pay it back?"

"How could I prove that?" Dad asked.

"By showing us that you already have the thousand dollars," said the bank officer.

"If I already *had* the thousand dollars, then why would I need to borrow it from *you*?" Dad asked.

"You're saying you don't have a thousand dollars?" asked the bank officer. His sunny disposition slid behind a cloud.

"No, of course I don't," said Dad.

"Well then, I'm afraid we can't take the chance of lending it to you," said the bank officer. He stood. "I'm sorry, Mr. Shluffmuffin."

Dad parked the car. This was not a part of Cincinnati that he had ever been to before. It was a seedy-looking neighborhood with older buildings, some of which had plywood panels in their windows instead of glass. A broken air conditioner, a dead TV, and an overstuffed armchair with stained upholstery had been left out on the curb. There was an odor of burnt maple syrup in the air.

Dad paused before a storefront that had the words PAWNSHOP and LOANS in flaking gold lettering on the window. He went inside.

The shop was loaded with an odd assortment of sad treasures that had once belonged to desperate people, things surrendered here in order to generate some cash and then never reclaimed. There were several guitars, a wide-brimmed cowboy hat, a battered bugle, a ten-speed bicycle, a tuxedo with comically wide lapels, and a glass display case littered with heaps of watches and jewelry.

A fellow wearing a green eyeshade, a scowl, and long floppy ears sat behind a counter, looking as if he'd eaten something that didn't agree with him. A troll.

"Yeah, what is it?" said the troll.

"I need a loan," said Dad.

The troll made a snorting sound in his nose. "You and everybody else on the planet, Chief," he said. "How much you need?"

"A thousand dollars."

The troll nodded. "The interest on that comes out to a hundred a week," he said.

"A hundred a *week*?" Dad repeated. "That's outrageous."

"Take it or leave it, *amigo,*" said the troll in a bored voice.

"Okay, okay," said Dad. "Do you need proof I already have a thousand?"

"Why would I need that?" asked the troll.

"So you can be sure I'll pay you back."

The troll laughed unpleasantly. "Oh, I'm not worried about *that,*" he said. "You'll pay me. If not, you'll wish you had. Gimme your driver's license."

Dad took out his wallet and handed the troll his license.

The troll passed Dad ten hundred-dollar bills.

"Thanks," said Dad. "When do you need this paid back?"

"I don't really care," said the troll. "Just keep paying me that hundred a week, and you can keep it as long as you like. Forever, for all I care."

"So how does it work?" Dad asked. "Am I supposed to come back here every week now and give you a hundred dollars, or what?"

The troll nodded. "If I don't have to come looking for you, *compadre,* you'll save yourself a lot of intense physical pain."

"I see," said Dad. "And when do I get my driver's license back?"

The troll just laughed.

When Dad returned to the Jolly Days Orphanage it was dark, and he no longer looked the same as he had eight hours earlier. He wore a glued-on bushy mustache and a dreadlocks wig. He knocked.

Hortense opened the door.

"Yes?" she said.

"Madame, my name ees Robaire," said Dad in a strange French accent. "My friend, Monsieur Shluffmuffin, he say come here eef I wish to adopt hees children. I have ze money."

"Really?" said Hortense. "How lovely! I am very pleasantly surprised. Is it the amount we . . .

That is to say, is it the same amount Mr. Shluffmuffin and I discussed?"

Dad nodded. He counted out fifteen hundred-dollar bills and gave them to her.

Hortense lit up like she'd been plugged into an electric socket.

"Come in, come in, Mr. Shl— I'm sorry, what are you calling yourself now?"

"Robaire," said Dad.

"Mr. Robaire," she repeated. "Cheyenne! Wally!" she called. "Your father's *friend* has come to get you."

Cheyenne and Wally came running.

"Dad!" shrieked Cheyenne.

"Dad!" shouted Wally.

Dad shook his head. "No-no-no, cheeldren. I am not ze dad," he said. "My name ees Robaire. I am ze *friend* of ze dad. Pack up your theengs and zen we go."

CHAPTER 4

It Turns Out You *Can* Go Home Again

When Dad drove Cheyenne and Wally back to the Spydelles', Shirley and Edgar greeted them at the front door. The twins threw themselves into Shirley's many arms, then shook hands warmly with Edgar.

"We're frightfully glad to have you back," said Edgar, puffing on his fragrant pipe. "It's been lonely as a boneyard here without you chaps."

"We missed you, too," said Wally.

Shirley shepherded them into the house. They all took seats at the dining table.

"For dinner tonight I've made you kids' favorite," said Shirley. "Jellied filet mignon."

"I can hardly wait," said Cheyenne.

Being a spider, Shirley injected all meat with her saliva, which predigested it into a kind of jelly. Shirley had not always been a spider, of course. When Edgar married her, she'd been a human. After a bite from a poisonous brown recluse spider, the life ebbed out of her, but Edgar brought her back from the dead with his Elixir of Life. His joy was only partly diminished when he discovered his invention had transformed her into a giant arachnid.

"Well, children," said Edgar, "good job you had your father to drive you today. If you'd taken a city bus, you might not have made it back here at all."

"What do you mean?" asked Wally.

"Haven't you heard the news?" asked Shirley. "Another busload of people in Cincinnati has disappeared."

"That makes four busloads so far," said Edgar.

"Where do they go?" asked Cheyenne.

"Nobody knows," said Edgar. "They just bloody vanish. Just like in the bloody Bermuda Triangle." He made a motion in the air with his right hand. *"Fffft.* Nearly three hundred people so far. Gone without a trace."

"You think it has anything to do with the Onts' plan to enslave mankind and end life on Earth as we know it?" asked Wally.

"I shouldn't be at all surprised," said Dad.

"Maybe we ought to go to the Ont Queen's cave tomorrow and check it out," said Wally.

"Oh no," said Dad. "Tomorrow you're going right back to Dripping Fang Country Day."

Both twins groaned.

"Why do we have to go back to that stupid school with all the freaks?" asked Wally.

"Because," said Dad, "if the Child Welfare Bureau finds I've taken you out of the orphanage, they're going to be mad because I don't have a job yet. Letting you skip school will tick them off even more."

"How'd you ever manage to get Hortense to let us go without paying her stupid adoption fee?" Cheyenne asked.

"What makes you think I didn't have to pay it?" said Dad.

"You actually paid her twelve hundred bucks to adopt us?" said Wally. "Where'd you get the money?"

"Oh, various places," said Dad. He picked up a knife off the table and studied his reflection in it, baring his fangs to make sure no spinach was stuck between them. "Edgar and Shirley were kind enough to give me some of it."

"And the rest?" said Cheyenne.

"Did you get it at the bank?" asked Shirley.

"Not exactly," said Dad.

"Then where?" asked Wally.

Satisfied that his teeth were spinach free, Dad put the knife back down on the table. "I borrowed it from a pawnshop," he said. "A troll gentleman lent it to me."

"You got it from a *troll*?" asked Wally. "Dad, those guys are the worst. They charge you tons of interest, and if you don't pay it, they break your kneecaps. How are you ever going to pay it back?"

"I don't know," said Dad. "But don't worry. I'll get a job somehow."

"But you haven't been able to get one so far," said Cheyenne.

"That's because people discover I'm a vampire, and then they don't want to hire me."

Dad hadn't always been a vampire, of course, and the twins hadn't always been orphans. Three years ago, when Dad was still a human, he'd taken Cheyenne and Wally to the circus. When Dad, a skinny gentleman, visited a circus Porta Potti, he fell in and drowned. Their mother, hoping to take their minds off this terrible tragedy, took them to a petting zoo, where a gang of crazed bunnies smothered her to death.

The twins were removed to the Jolly Days Orphanage, and Dad became a zombie due to drowning in the Porta Potti. It was Edgar's Elixir of Life that had cured him of zombiism, but sadly also transformed him into a vampire.

"Maybe you should stop pretending you aren't a vampire," said Wally. "Maybe you should try to get a job where they *want* somebody who has fangs and wings and longs to drink human blood."

"You mean be a freak at a carnival side-show?" said Dad.

"Yeah," said Cheyenne. "Or get a part in a vampire movie or something."

"I think that's a great idea," said Wally.

"Hmmm," said Dad.

CHAPTER 5

The Vampire Movie Sounds Interesting, But the Part Sucks

There was no sign on the frosted-glass-paneled door, so when Dad walked into the tiny office, he didn't know if he was in the right place.

"Excuse me," said Dad to the blond man in a black T-shirt and jeans who was sitting behind a desk littered with stacks of photos. "Is this where you're holding auditions for *Die, Innocent Teenagers, Die*?"

"Yes, won't you come in?" said the blond man. His voice seemed surprisingly resonant, as though he were doing a commercial for expensive foreign cars.

"Thank you," said Dad.

"And you're here to read for the part of . . . ?"

"Yergin, the vampire," said Dad. He took out the coffee-stained pages from the script that he'd been rehearsing.

"Oh yes. Of course," said the blond man. "I'm afraid I have some bad news, though. The part of Yergin the vampire has already been cast."

"Oh," said Dad. He couldn't hide his disappointment.

"I'm sorry," said the blond man. "We still do have a few parts open. Would you like to read for the part of the zombie?"

"The zombie?" said Dad. "Uh, well, yes, I suppose I could do that. As a matter of fact, I've even had some experience as a zombie."

"Is that so?" said the blond man. "In a movie or on TV?"

"Neither one," said Dad.

"Oh, on the stage?" said the blond man. "In a production I might have seen, perhaps?"

"I don't think you would have seen me," said

Dad. "Look, it doesn't matter. Where in the script does the zombie part begin?"

"It begins on page forty-three," said the blond man. "It also ends on page forty-three. I'm afraid

it's only one line. Here," he said, holding out a sheaf of pages stapled together. "You can read it right off my script. Take a look at it, and then, whenever you're ready, just say the line out loud."

Dad looked at the line, then read it out loud without any expression: "Want flesh, must consume dead flesh."

"Uh-huh," said the blond man. "Look, I know that was a cold reading, so maybe it wasn't fair. But what I'm getting from you, frankly, is very little zombie and a whole lot of vampire. Why don't you take another shot at it, and this time try to forget you came to read for the vampire part and give me all you've got as a zombie. Really sell me on the fact that you're a zombie, okay? Ready . . . and . . . *action!*"

"Want flesh," Dad read with the same lack of expression, "must consume dead flesh."

"Uh-huh," said the blond man. "Well, thank you. And, hey, thanks for coming in. Leave us your number, and we'll call you."

"Tell me the truth," said Dad. "Do I have a chance?"

"My advice?" said the blond man. "Don't give up your day job."

"I don't *have* a day job," said Dad.

"Then maybe you ought to get one," said the blond man.

CHAPTER 6

The Adoption Process Can Often Be Such a Heartache

When Hortense heard the knock at the front door, at first she decided not to answer it. She knew who it was, of course—the Stumpfs—and she wasn't eager to tell them they couldn't have the twins after all. They might be a tad upset, but they'd get over it. Maybe she'd offer them a couple of the other orphans—Wayne and Orville. Wayne still had the teensiest tendency to set fires when bored, and Orville didn't quite have that pooping-in-his-pants problem entirely solved. It would be nice to get rid of them.

There was more knocking. Why not just get it over with, Hortense decided. She opened the door.

"We've come for the children," said Mrs. Stumpf. She smelled vaguely of thick brown gravy.

"There's been a slight problem," said Hortense.

"How slight a problem?" asked Mrs. Stumpf.

"Due to unforeseen circumstances, I was forced to release them to another adopter," said Hortense.

"But we signed papers," said Mr. Stumpf. "We even gave you a check."

"Under certain circumstances, checks can be partially refunded," said Hortense.

Both Mr. and Mrs. Stumpf burst into tears.

"Or wholly refunded," added Hortense quickly.

"Who adopted them?" sobbed Mrs. Stumpf.

"I'm sorry," said Hortense, "but the privacy laws prevent me from revealing that information. Please don't cry."

"W-we l-l-loved those ch-ch-children," said Mr. Stumpf, his eyes and nose beginning to leak. "Wh-who ad-d-dopted them?"

"Will you please stop this crying," said Hortense.

Mr. and Mrs. Stumpf wailed with grief. They blubbered uncontrollably, tears splashing down their cheeks and chins and cascading onto their chests like a mountain brook over a waterfall.

"I don't suppose it would be a violation of privacy to say that the adopter was their natural father, Mr. Sheldon Shluffmuffin, who is currently residing at the home of Professor and Mrs. Spydelle in Dripping Fang Forest," said Hortense.

CHAPTER 7

What Is This Thing You've Got Against Ghouls?

When Cheyenne and Wally walked back into the classroom at Dripping Fang Country Day, the kids all turned around in their seats and stared. They were the same freaks who'd taunted the twins when they had been there before—the three-foot-long giant slug, the six wolf cubs, the two trolls with red buzz cuts and floppy ears, the young ghoul with saggy white cheeks and sharp yellow teeth, and the boy whose eyes were located at the ends of stalks growing out of his forehead. All, of course, wore the Dripping Fang Country Day School uniform of black blazers and tan slacks or skirts.

Standing at the large green blackboard was their teacher, Mrs. McCaw, a woman with a large birdlike beak where her nose and mouth should have been.

"Well," she said, "what a nice surprise. Welcome back, Studmuppets. Where have you been?"

"It's a long story," said Wally.

"Tell us," said Mrs. McCaw in her screechy parrotlike voice. "We love long stories."

Wally looked at Cheyenne.

"The Child Welfare Bureau took us away from our dad because he doesn't have a job," said Cheyenne. "So we had to go back to the orphanage."

"Then two ghouls tried to adopt us," said Wally, "but Dad borrowed money from a troll and bribed the orphanage owner to let us go."

"Why did you say two *ghouls* tried to adopt you?" asked the kid with triangular yellow teeth. "Why didn't you just say two *people* tried to adopt you? What have you got against ghouls?"

"I don't know," said Wally. "Maybe I'm just

ARE YOU A MUTANT?
-DO YOU HAVE FANGS?
-IS YOUR DAD A SLUG?
-DO YOU HAVE FUR?
-DO YOU LIKE EATING HUMANS?

prejudiced against people who want to eat my flesh."

"Then are you prejudiced against your father, who wants to drink your blood?" asked the kid with the triangular yellow teeth.

"He doesn't want to drink *our* blood, you moron," said Wally.

"Who are you calling a moron, you moron?" said the kid with triangular yellow teeth.

"All right, children, that will be quite enough," said Mrs. McCaw.

"At least their father's a vampire," said the boy with eyes at the end of stalks growing out of his forehead. "These kids don't look like a vampire's kids, though. They look like anybody in Cincinnati—they look like freaks."

"Children . . . ," said Mrs. McCaw.

"Maybe they look normal under their clothes," said one of the troll kids.

"Yeah," said one of the wolf kids. "Let's take off their clothes and see."

The kids in class began to get excited. "Take off their clothes! Take off their clothes!" they chanted as they closed in on Cheyenne and Wally and began tugging at their uniforms.

"Children!" screeched Mrs. McCaw.

Although the twins fought back bravely, the kids managed to pull Wally's pants and Cheyenne's skirt down around their ankles and had started on their underpants when Mrs. McCaw's ruler began whacking at their butts.

CHAPTER 8

We'd Like You to Consider a Few of the Advantages of Eternal Life

"Try to stand still," said Dad. "At least until the glue sets."

"How long do you think that will be?" asked Cheyenne.

"I don't know," said Dad. "About five minutes, I think. It says on the tube."

Cheyenne and Wally had their T-shirts pulled up in back and were bent over, with their hands on the Spydelles' kitchen table. Dad was trying to attach small leathery wings to their shoulder blades with Krazy Glue. The fumes from the glue were almost as bad as the ammonia they'd used to scrub tiles at the orphanage.

"I'm not so sure this is a great idea, Dad," said Wally.

"I know," said Dad. "Krazy Glue is bad for your skin. But we'll take it off tomorrow night with nail polish remover as soon as the kids see you have wings."

"No, I meant, do you really think gluing these things on is going to convince anybody we're vampires?"

"Probably not," said Dad. "The only convincing way would be for me to bite you both on the neck and make you immortal. You might want to consider that, by the way. Being a vampire isn't too bad a life. Try to hold still if you can."

"If I were a vampire, would I stay the same age or would I grow older?" asked Wally.

"Good question," said Dad. "I don't think I know the answer, though. Why, which would you prefer?"

"Well, I certainly wouldn't want to stay the same age," said Wally. "I mean, who'd want to have zits for hundreds of years?"

"If we could grow to teen age and stay there for a few centuries, that might not be too bad," said Cheyenne. "I'd love to wear makeup and stockings and high heels and watch the centuries pass by. Go to other planets and find out if there's intelligent life. See if mankind can ever stop having wars. See what happens when the glaciers melt. Stuff like that. You know, becoming a vampire could definitely be an interesting experience."

Dad held Wally's wings in place and squeezed out a little more glue. Wally wrinkled his nose.

"It would be lovely to have you guys with me forever, though, watching history unfold," said Dad dreamily. "Nobody could ever kill us or separate us. We'd be the Indestructible Three, something like superheroes."

"*Vampire* superheroes, though," said Cheyenne.

"True," said Dad. "But think of the good times we'd have, the adventures. Whereas, if you remain human, I'm going to have to watch you grow up, gradually overtake me in age, and eventually get old and die, leaving me all alone."

"*Aww,* poor Dad," said Wally.

When Dad knocked on the door of the apartment where he'd been told the party would be, he wondered if there'd been a mistake. From the racket he could hear on the other side of the door, it sounded as though the building were being demolished by forty chimpanzees and a wrecking ball. He rang the bell insistently, and eventually the door was opened by a frazzled-looking woman.

"Oh, there you are," said the frazzled woman. "Thank heavens! The children were getting a little impatient. Good, I see you came in costume. Come in, come in, and we'll get started."

The frazzled woman led Dad into the apartment. Three dozen youngsters were having a food fight with what was left of a large birthday cake and individual ice-cream sundaes.

"Kids, guess what!" shouted the frazzled

woman. "Our vampire has arrived! Isn't that exciting?"

The kids stopped throwing food and looked at Dad.

"Who are *you* supposed to be?" asked a freckled boy. He had ice cream in his hair and in one nostril.

"I am Count Tibor, Vampire King of Transylvania," said Dad in a vaguely Hungarian accent. "Ohhhhhh, very scary, boys and girls, very scary!" He stretched his wings, bared his fangs, and made a terrible howling noise: *"Arrrooooooooo!"*

"If you're a vampire," said the boy, "then I'm a kangaroo." He made a fart noise with his mouth.

This was going to be a *long* party.

ADVANTAGES AND DISADVANTAGES
OF BECOMING A VAMPIRE
By Cheyenne Shluffmuffin, Extra-Credit
Think Piece, Mrs. McCaw's Class

ADVANTAGE: Vampires live forever. This is cool because dying is a drag, and I still have no proof that there is an afterlife, even though I have asked for proof on several occasions. Also, you'd save money on funerals and coffins and stuff, which could be a lot.

DISADVANTAGE: Vampires have to drink human blood. I tasted human blood once. I accidentally cut my finger, and I sucked on it to get it clean, which is what you have to do if you don't want to get an infection. It tasted okay but kind of metallic and not really all that good, if you want to know the truth, and remember, this was just a drop or two. Imagine if you had to drink whole entire _glassfuls_ of it and that was all you could drink, no cold lemonade or hot apple cider or chocolate milk shakes or anything else. I mean, wouldn't that suck?

ADVANTAGE: Vampires don't get older. I do want to get a _little_ older, but not _really_ old, like thirty or forty, so not getting older could be a definite plus. I do plan to fall in love someday and get married and have kids and all that stuff. So, if I became a vampire, I hope I wouldn't screw THAT up, because ten is definitely too young to do any of those things. On second thought, this could be a <u>disadvantage</u>.

DISADVANTAGE: Vampires can be killed by a wooden stake or by a silver bullet through the heart. Well, except for Dad, of course. When Dad mistakenly thought Wally and I were dead and he was so depressed he tried to commit suicide, neither of those worked for him because the wooden stake turned out to be not real wood but Formica and the bullet turned out to be silver <u>plate</u>--which I'm glad about, of course, don't get me wrong, but it must have been pretty frustrating for Dad. I mean, if a person really feels bad enough to commit suicide, he should be able to do it and it shouldn't be so hard that he would get discouraged.

ADVANTAGE: Vampires can't be killed by normal things like machetes, bombs, bullets that aren't silver, or a safe falling on your head. (Actually, I'll have to check on the safe thing to be sure, although I don't think so.) This comes in handy in today's world, where we are constantly being menaced by drunken drivers, wars, terrorists, bird flu, and boys with eyes on the ends of stalks growing out of their foreheads.

DISADVANTAGE: Vampires seem to wear capes a lot, at least in horror movies. I wouldn't want to have to wear a cape, which would probably be heavy and too warm in the summer, although in winter one might be kind of nice.

ADVANTAGE: Vampires can fly. Dad doesn't really do too much of this, but he could if he wanted to, I think. I'd love to fly, and I don't mean on an airliner where they don't even give you lunch anymore, just peanuts or pretzels in a little blue-foil bag, which is hardly lunch. I mean, sometimes I'd like to fly like a bird and just ride the upward drafts, which I think are called thermals, coasting and relaxing and looking down at the tiny people and buildings on the ground. It would be like you were dreaming, except with no drooling onto your pillow.

DISADVANTAGE: Vampires scare a lot of people. I don't see why, because judging by my dad, they are really gentle and sweet and wouldn't ever hurt you, but like I said, a lot of people get bummed out by the fangs and wings and stuff, so this could be a barrier if you're trying to make a boy who you just met like you or when you want to make new friends at school, except in the case of Dripping Fang Country Day, of course, where if you're NOT weird they're all over you and in your face.

All in all, I guess there are maybe slightly more <u>disadvantages</u> than <u>advantages</u> in being a vampire.

Dad was taking an afternoon snooze in the Spydelles' living-room hammock when he gradually became aware that somebody was standing quite close to him. He opened his eyes and was startled to see the troll from the pawnshop.

"How did you get in here?" Dad asked.

"That's not important, Mr. Shluffmuffin," said the troll, pulling on his fingers and cracking his knuckles. "What *is* important is that you have failed to pay your first week's interest on your loan."

"Oh, sorry," said Dad. "I meant to, I really did, but I've been so busy trying to get work to pay you that I haven't had the time."

"You haven't had the *time,* Mr. Shluffmuffin?" said the troll with a sneer.

"That's right, I haven't, no."

"Then may I suggest that you *find* the time, Mr. Shluffmuffin?"

The troll grabbed Dad painfully by one ear, pulled him out of the hammock, and forced him to his knees on the floor.

"Hey, that hurts!" said Dad.

"It's *supposed* to hurt, Mr. Shluffmuffin," said the troll. He gave Dad's ear an especially hard yank and then released it. "If you hurt people, sometimes it helps them remember to do the things they promised. I shall return, Mr. Shluffmuffin. Do not doubt that for a minute. And if you have not paid what you owe me, next time I may not be quite so understanding."

CHAPTER 9

It's Enough to Make an Insect Puke

The clearing in the woods in front of the Ont Queen's cave was a hubbub of activity. Although it was night, bluish-white floodlights mounted on high steel tripods painted the area almost as bright as day.

Several city buses—Cheyenne and Wally couldn't tell how many—were parked a short distance from the mouth of the cave. Dozens of female ont guards in camouflage fatigues were striding up and down on the narrow patches of matted grass between the buses. One of them was yelling through a battery-powered police bullhorn, the sound rolling and bouncing off the rock formations and echoing in the cool night air.

"Attention on the buses!" yelled the guard. "You are now prisoners of the Ont Queen of Ohio! If you do exactly as you're told, you will not be harmed!"

The onts' shiny black insect faces, with their compound eyes, antennae, and mandibles that looked like large black pliers mounted sideways, appeared even more grotesque in the glare and shadow of the floodlights.

"This is really creepy," whispered Cheyenne.

"Ssshhhh," warned Wally, putting a finger to his lips.

The twins were crouching behind a large boulder at least fifty feet from the clearing. With all the activity going on in front of them, it was unlikely they'd be noticed.

"First of all," continued the ont guard on the echoing bullhorn, "a few words about the superiority of insects. There are more species of insects on earth than all other animals put together. Ninety-five percent of all animal species on the earth are insects! Not only do we far outnumber you, but most insects can fly, which you pitiful humans cannot. We are also superior in hearing, smelling, and strength: The average human can pull his own weight, but an ant can pull fifty-two *times* her own weight—that would be like a human pulling four and a half tons.

"There have been insects on earth for over three hundred million years—cockroaches have been here even longer than dinosaurs. You humans have been here—what? A puny hundred thousand years? And even *you* admit that when you finally kill yourselves off in a stupid thermonuclear war, the only survivors will be insects.

"So how do you honor a superior species? By worshipping us the way the ancient Egyptians worshipped cats? No! By practicing genocide on us: Ant traps! Bug bombs! Raid! Roach Motels—'Roaches check in . . . but they don't check out!' And if killing us isn't barbaric enough, you humans *eat* over a thousand species of us!"

The ant guard shuddered.

"Humans in Mexico eat fried grasshoppers and chocolate-covered ants. Humans in Colombia eat termites and palm grubs—ants are ground up and used as a spread on breads. Humans in the Philippines eat June beetles, grasshoppers, ants, mole crickets, water beetles, katydids, locusts, and dragonfly larvae. Humans in Africa eat ants, termites, beetle grubs, caterpillars, and grasshoppers. In Asia the giant water bug is roasted and eaten whole. In the United States, humans not only eat *grown-up* grasshoppers, cicadas, stick insects,

moths, and crickets but also defenseless *baby* moths, wasps, butterflies, dragonflies, and beetles. It's enough to make an insect puke!

"Well, my friends, all that's about to change!" yelled the guard. "Starting tonight the master species begins calling the shots. Those of you who choose to recognize us as your masters, we'll put you to work and take good care of you, just as we take care of our herds of nectar-producing aphids. Those of you who don't . . . Well, we'll find another use for you that you might not find as pleasant. Now, begin filing quietly out of your buses in an orderly manner, and follow the guards into the cave."

The doors of the buses swung open on small sighs of compressed air. People began stepping cautiously out of the buses, some more readily than others, some of them sobbing quietly. They tried not to look at their grotesque captors.

"We've got to tell somebody about this!" whispered Cheyenne.

"Yeah, but who'd believe us?" whispered Wally.

Twenty feet behind the twins, heavy shrubbery hid two huge shadowy shapes.

"Those Shluffmuffin twins are totally focused on the onts," said Wolfgang Stumpf. "If we grabbed them now, we'd catch them completely unawares."

"I know, Poopsie," said Fritzi Stumpf. "But this is not the moment. We still have much planning to do."

"And recipes to be worked out," said Mr. Stumpf.

CHAPTER 10

I'm Sorry, But Burping the Alphabet Is *Not* on Our List of Approved Artistic Achievements

The tiny waiting room where Dad was sitting was barely big enough to hold a desk, much less the tiny receptionist *behind* the desk who looked so fragile she'd shatter at the sound of a really loud noise. Opposite the reception desk was a tiny vinyl-covered couch with stuffing coming out of rips in the cushions. On the wall were framed posters of carnival acts featuring fire-eaters, tiger tamers, and bearded ladies.

"Next!" called the voice on the other side of the door.

"You may go in now," whispered the tiny receptionist.

"Thanks," Dad whispered. He opened the door and entered the office.

The man behind the desk wore wide red suspenders, a polka-dot bow tie, and a narrow-brimmed straw hat perched on top of his head. A cigar that had long since gone out was wedged into the side of his mouth. He was leaning back in a chair with both hands clasped behind his head.

"Okay, fella, what's your gimmick?" asked the man. "No, don't tell me, *show* me."

In reply Dad silently removed his jacket, took off his shirt, flexed his leathery wings, and bared his fangs.

The man behind the desk studied him silently for sixty seconds, then said, "Okay, but what do you do?"

"What do you mean, what do I do?" Dad asked.

"I mean, do you also walk on your hands, balance spoons on your nose, juggle flaming torches, handle rattlesnakes, swallow live hamsters—anything like that? I'm looking for a gimmick here."

"No," said Dad. "The fangs and the wings are pretty much all I've got. I thought that would be enough of a gimmick."

"You mean to tell me there's nothing you know how to *do*?" said the man.

"Well," said Dad, "I do know how to do orthodontics."

"Ortho *what*?"

"Orthodontics," said Dad. "I straighten teeth. I make dental retainers and braces, that sort of thing."

The man behind the desk took the cigar out of his mouth, studied it intently as if he hadn't seen it before, then shoved it back in his face.

"Okay, pal," said the man, "I'll tellya what. I'll stick you in a booth at the carnival, and we'll give it a shot for a couple of days. You'll just stand there with your fangs and your wings, and we'll see how they like you. Fair enough?"

"I guess so," said Dad.

"Great," said the man. "Next!"

CHAPTER 11

For Conspiracies Involving Giant Mealworms You Need to Go to a Different Department

"Yes, may I help you?" asked the FBI receptionist. She wore black-rimmed glasses and a headset. On her desk were a phone and a clipboard. The great seal of the Federal Bureau of Investigation hovered over her head like a giant halo.

"Yes," said Cheyenne. "We want to talk to somebody about a problem."

"And what kind of problem would this be?" asked the receptionist.

"A problem of somebody plotting to enslave mankind and end life on Earth as we know it," said Wally.

"I see," said the receptionist. She consulted

her clipboard. "And would these plotting parties be . . . giant ants?"

"How did you know that?" said Cheyenne.

"I remember you from the last time you were here," said the receptionist. "Would you like to speak to one of our agents?"

"Yes, thanks," said Wally.

"Just a moment, please." She buzzed somebody on her intercom.

"Sir," she said, "there are two children here who wish assistance with giant ants plotting to enslave mankind and end life on Earth as we know it. Yes, sir. I'll send them right in." She turned to the twins. "Down the hall to room 2059."

"Thank you," said Cheyenne.

Cheyenne and Wally walked down the long hallway past many offices filled with khaki-colored metal filing cabinets. The offices smelled like piles of mildewed newspapers. Finally, they arrived at room 2059.

A man sat behind a desk, busily eating pistachio nuts from a silver bowl. He had a too-perfect tan and white hair that looked like it had been sprayed till it was a hard shell. "Hi there," said the man. "I'm Special Agent Tom Cromwell."

"Hi," said Wally. "We're the Shluffmuffins, Cheyenne and Wally."

"You kids have been here before, haven't you?" said Cromwell. "You were the ones who made up that marvelous put-on about the giant ants who were going to enslave mankind or something, right?"

"Right," said Wally, "but it wasn't a put-on, sir. These giant ants really *are* plotting to enslave mankind. We came to tell you that they've already started. You heard about those busloads of people that disappeared from downtown Cincinnati? Well, the giant ants are the ones who did that."

"Marvelous," said Cromwell. "Simply marvelous." He chuckled and carefully removed the shells from several pistachio nuts.

"We're serious, sir," said Cheyenne. "We can tell you exactly where to find the buses, and all the people who were on them."

"This isn't a joke?" said Cromwell.

"No, sir," said Cheyenne.

"Okay," said Cromwell, "where are they?"

"In Dripping Fang Forest, sir, on the outskirts of the city," said Wally. "In a clearing in the woods, outside a huge cave. Do you have access to satellite photographs?"

"Of course."

"Well, if you can zero in on Dripping Fang Forest, you ought to be able to see the buses. If you show us the satellite photographs, we could point them out."

"Totally out of the question," said Cromwell. "That's top secret stuff."

"Really?" said Wally. "Too bad. We could have shown you exactly where the buses are."

"*Aaahh,* what the heck," said Cromwell. "Let's go take a look. Follow me."

Cromwell spread the satellite photos out on a table like a paper tablecloth at a picnic. They presented an aerial view of Dripping Fang Forest.

Cheyenne and Wally bent over the photos and studied them.

"This is the highway that goes to the forest," said Wally. "This is the road that runs through it."

"This is the Spydelles' house, where we live," said Cheyenne. "And this is the clearing next to the cave where the buses . . . That's weird. When was this picture taken?"

"This morning," said Cromwell. "Why?"

"The buses are gone," said Wally.

Cromwell raised his eyebrows. "Gone?" he asked. "Or never there?"

Wally and Cheyenne moved slowly through the bushes. The sun was hot, and sweat was rolling down their foreheads and down their chests and backs inside their T-shirts. Tiny flies and mosquitoes whined annoyingly in their ears.

Ahead of them was the Ont Queen's cave, and beyond that the clearing where the buses had been the night before.

"The buses *are* gone," whispered Cheyenne. "Where do you think they put them?"

"I don't know," said Wally. "If they drove

them out of the forest, somebody would have seen them."

The twins crept forward warily, on the alert for the first sign of guards. They saw no one.

"Look," said Cheyenne, pointing.

Wally looked.

In the grass was a deep indentation that was at least fifty feet long. They followed the indentation along the ground and saw that it made a ninety-degree turn. After another twenty feet, it made another ninety-degree turn. The indentation was actually a huge rectangular shape in the grass.

"What is this thing?" whispered Cheyenne.

"It's bigger than a bus," said Wally. "It's bigger than *two* buses! I bet it's some kind of an elevator. I bet this whole thing lowers down into the ground, and that's how they got rid of the buses—into some kind of underground garage."

CHAPTER 12

You Folks Have Been a Great Audience—I'll Be Here All Week

There were only three people in the tiny tent—two middle-aged women and a skinny gentleman of about ninety who wore a loose-fitting electric-blue nylon shirt and brown slacks that were a foot too short. The old man was humming. The two women were chewing gum.

A man wearing a straw hat, red suspenders, and a polka-dot bow tie walked into the tent, carrying a megaphone. Although there were only three people there, he raised the megaphone to his lips.

"Ladies and gentlemen!" said the man in a singsong voice. "Children of all ages! Are you ready to be amazed, amused, astonished, astounded, and thrilled to the very marrow of your bones? Are you prepared to have your eyes deceive you and the blood in your veins run so cold as to make frost form on your skin?"

"Sure, why not?" said one of the middle-aged ladies. Her friend snorted with laughter.

"Good," said the man in the straw hat. "Because I am about to present to you the newest attraction in the Max Marvel Marvelous Midway of Freaks and Monsters. Ladies and gentlemen, I give you now the terrifying and bloodthirsty vampire of darkest Transylvania . . . Count Tibor the Terrible!"

The man turned on a small cassette recorder. It played a tinny fanfare. He reached upward and pulled a cord that opened a red velvet curtain, and then he left the tent.

On a small dark stage three feet off the floor stood a tall figure shrouded in a black velvet cape. With a dramatic flourish, the figure snapped open its cape. It was Dad in a black tank top and jogging pants. He spread out his leathery wings

to their full extension, bared his fangs, and snarled a terrible snarl.

"Oh boy," said one of the women dryly, "I can feel the frost forming on my skin already."

Her companion giggled.

"I'm not even mildly frightened, are you?" said the first woman. "Would a real vampire dress like that? I mean, check out those fangs. And the wings? Give me a *break*. Could they look any cheesier?"

Her companion shook her head.

"You feel that my fangs and wings are not genuine, madam?" Dad asked.

Both women giggled.

"Right," said the one who'd spoken.

"Then would you care to come up here and examine them?"

"Sure, why not?" said the woman. She walked up the three wooden steps to the stage.

"Do not be afraid to approach me," said Dad.

"Afraid?" said the woman. "Why would I be afraid?"

"All right, madam, now take a close look at my fangs," said Dad. "Tell me what you see there." He bared his fangs and drew his lips away from his gums in a grimace.

"Well, for one thing, I see that you don't floss," said the woman. "I see spinach and maybe a little broccoli."

"What else?"

"I see somebody's gone to an awful lot of trouble to make you a bridge with fake fangs."

"All right, madam, now take a close look at my wings." Dad whirled and showed her his back.

"Hmmm," said the woman. "Well, here again, somebody's gone to an awful lot of trouble to make those wings look authentic."

"You're still not convinced I'm authentic," said Dad. He was annoyed. "Why don't you take my pulse, madam? Do you know how to take a pulse?"

"I'd *better* know how to take a pulse," said the woman. "I happen to be a registered nurse."

"Good," said Dad, getting steamed. "Then take my pulse, nursie."

She took Dad's wrist in a swift professional grip. She frowned. "That's odd," she said. She put three fingers on his neck along his carotid artery. Her frown deepened. "How did you stop your pulse? Is it a yogi thing or what?"

"It is not a yogi thing, madam," said Dad, controlling his anger with difficulty. "It is a *dead* thing. I do not have a pulse because I am not alive."

With that he grabbed her wrist and bit it. Had he just created another vampire? He didn't care.

The woman screamed and ran out of the tent. She was followed by the other woman and the old man.

From somewhere nearby came the sound of a solitary person clapping. The man with the straw hat, the red suspenders, and the polka-dot bow tie came into the tent, clapping.

"I don't blame you for doing that," said the

man. "On the other hand, we can't have you chewing on the customers. Tellya what. You can work the rest of the week, but no more chewing on the customers, okay?"

"Okay," said Dad.

CHAPTER 13

School for Mutants

It was night in the dark forest. The only sounds were the wind sighing through the thick trees and the occasional twittering of a bird that had awakened, believing it to be morning.

Cheyenne moaned in her sleep. She was having a nightmare about being held captive on a bus by giant cockroaches. They reached out for her with enormous claws, and she cried out and jolted into wakefulness. For a moment she thought she was still on the bus with the cock-roaches. Then she realized she was safe in her bed at the Spydelles'. She could hear Wally snoring softly in his bed. Suddenly a dark shape moved outside the bedroom window. Cheyenne sat up.

There was definitely somebody or *something* outside the bedroom. Now a big white sign appeared in the window. The thick black letters read: WOULD YOU LIKE TO MEET THE BABIES?

Cheyenne had no idea what this meant, and yet the words seemed strangely familiar. They sizzled onto her pupils like a branding iron, then sank through her eyeballs and went deep into her brain. Her body relaxed, and she slipped into a light trance.

Wally mumbled something in his sleep, then awoke abruptly and opened his eyes. Cheyenne was standing beside her bed, looking dazed, and Wally realized what was going on.

"Cheyenne, wake up!" Wally whispered.

She shuddered and popped out of her trance.

"What th—?"

"*Sssshhh.* Cheyenne, listen to me," Wally whispered. "I just woke you out of a trance, okay? The Ont Queen has sent someone to take you back to her cave. Do you understand what I'm telling you? Don't answer out loud. Whisper."

"I understand what you're telling me," Cheyenne whispered. "What should we do?"

"I hate to even suggest this, Cheyenne," said Wally, "because I know what you had to go through the last time, but if you could stand to go back there again and pretend you're still hypnotized . . . Well, it would really help. You could check out what happened to the buses and the people who were on them. Maybe you could take along a camera this time. Maybe even take some pictures of the buses or the guys they captured."

Cheyenne thought about what she'd had to endure the last time she'd gone to the Ont Queen's cave while pretending to be in a trance. She thought about the tests that nasty little mutant Betsy had put Cheyenne through to see if she was faking—making her drink the mutants' spit out of a glass, then biting Cheyenne and forcing her to pretend she didn't feel the pain. Cheyenne hadn't thought she could do it, but somehow she did. And she could probably stand to do it again.

"Do we have a really small camera?" she asked.

"Yeah," said Wally, "that little digital one of Shirley's."

"Get it for me and I'll go," she said.

The walk through the silent forest with Cheyenne's nonspeaking black-hatted ont escort was about the same as last time. So was the ritual of going through security with the guards at the mouth of the cave. And so was the brief audience in the glitter-domed throne room of the Ont Queen, with the gold-plated stalactites and stalagmites, the thousand flickering candles in the black wrought-iron candelabra, and the whale-sized queen reclining on a ninety-foot-long royal sofa. Now for the part Cheyenne dreaded most: going into that classroom with the mutant kids.

"Attention, children!" said Hedy Mandible through the mask that hid the part of her face that had been hideously disfigured in the Mandible House fire.

Twenty mutant children stopped fighting

long enough to stare at the human girl that Hedy had led into the classroom. The mutants—half ont, half human, the unplanned result of having been fed human snot during their larval stage—with their grotesque ant features covered in human skin, were hard for even onts to look at.

"We are fortunate tonight to have another visit from Cheyenne Shluffmuffin," Hedy continued. "She is once more in a hypnotic trance, but as you know she's still able to speak to us. Tonight she'll begin to teach us things about humans that will assist us in making better slaves out of them."

"Can we get her to do more disgusting things like drink our spit?" asked Betsy.

"No, Betsy," said Hedy.

"*Aww,* why not?" asked Betsy.

"Because that serves no purpose," said Hedy. "We're here tonight to learn about humans, not to torture the human who teaches us."

"I'm here to do both," said Betsy.

"Well, fine," said Hedy, "but not on *my* time. Now, despite the fact that we've begun to transfer humans from downtown Cincinnati to our underground headquarters here, we need a plan to infiltrate human communities all over the country where we can do the same. This is where you children can be valuable."

"Drop us off in neighborhoods all over Ohio, and we'll destroy everything in sight," said a mutant named Diane. She was bigger than the other children, and hideous fangs protruded from her plierslike jaws.

"Thank you, Diane," said Hedy. "Actually, we had a little more devious idea than that in mind. We're going to get humans to adopt you, and—"

"Adopt us?" shouted a mutant named Janet. "We *refuse* to be adopted by humans!"

All the mutants started yelling and pounding the desks. Hedy emitted a piercing shriek that hurt their ears and calmed them down.

"Please do not do that again or I shall have to take even more unpleasant measures to silence you," said Hedy. "What I meant by *adopted* is not what you think. We intend to infiltrate human families by getting them to 'adopt' mutant onts. Once inside these new families, mutant children will destroy them from within by several means that we will teach you."

"Who'd adopt *us*?" asked Betsy. "Humans will think we're ugly. They won't even be able to stand to look at us."

"That's the beauty of our plan," said Hedy. "Most humans will adopt anything if they pity it enough. When a mother cat saved her kittens from a barn fire and got severely burned and disfigured in the process, humans declared her a hero. They *stampeded* to adopt her. Now, Cheyenne here is an orphan who knows something about the adoption process. I want her to tell us how to make humans eager to adopt you. Cheyenne?"

Cheyenne thought this over, then began speaking in what she hoped sounded like the voice of somebody in a trance.

"Humans like it when you're very polite," she said. "Humans like it when you say *please* and *thank you* and *sir* and *ma'am*."

"How do we inspire pity in them?" asked Betsy.

"Act helpless," said Cheyenne. "Make them feel protective toward you. Act grateful if they show you the slightest bit of kindness."

"That will make me vomit," said Betsy.

"Do you want to get adopted or don't you?" Cheyenne asked.

"Good advice, Cheyenne," said Hedy. "Children, have you seen the adoption vans that animal shelters use? They'll drive into a neighborhood with a bunch of dogs and cats in the van. People come to look at them in the vans, feel sorry for them, and then adopt them. That's what we'll be doing with *you.*"

"What are we supposed to do once they adopt us?" asked Diane.

"Do you know what cuckoos do?" asked Hedy.

"Yeah," said Betsy. "They jump out of clocks and go 'Cuckoo! Cuckoo!'"

Everybody laughed.

"Cuckoo *birds,*" said Hedy, "lay their own,

larger eggs in other birds' nests when the parents are out looking for food. Then when the cuckoos' eggs hatch, the baby cuckoos, which are larger and smarter, steal food from the parent birds' real children and will even throw them out of the nest and kill them, if necessary.

"We want you children to become our cuckoos."

The mutants cheered and banged their desks.

CHAPTER 14

The Enemy of My Enemy Is My Friend

When the class was over, the mutants had a brief fight with blackboard erasers, creating puffs of chalk dust. Then all but Betsy left the classroom.

"Hedy, who's escorting Cheyenne back to her home?" Betsy asked.

"One of the black-hats," said Hedy.

"Let *me* do it tonight," said Betsy.

"That's not your job," said Hedy. "It's a black-hat job."

"But tonight *I* want to do it," said Betsy.

"I'd have to get you permission," said Hedy.

"Okay, you do that," said Betsy.

Hedy left the classroom. Betsy strolled up to Cheyenne.

"I don't really want to walk you home," said Betsy. "I just needed to get her out of here so I could talk to you alone. I want to tell you that you don't fool me."

Wisely, Cheyenne said nothing.

"The last time you were here," said Betsy, "I knew you were faking being in a trance. I don't like you, but I respect the fact that you forced yourself to drink our spit and to let me bite you without flinching."

Cheyenne continued to say nothing. *This is a trick,* she thought, *another test to see if I'm only pretending to be in a trance.*

"You think I'm trying to trick you, don't you?" said Betsy. "I could be, but I'm not. I've got something a lot more important to talk to you about. I know you don't like me, either, and I can't say I blame you, but I think we can work together anyway. 'The enemy of my enemy is my friend,' as some guy once said. Truth is, I could use your help. I have big plans. Want to hear what they are?"

Cheyenne didn't react at all.

"I plan to be the queen here someday," said Betsy. "Someday soon."

Is this a joke, or is she crazy? Probably both.

"You think that's crazy—a kid like me as queen?" Betsy asked. "Well, it's not. Do you know your history, Cheyenne? Have you heard of Louis the Fourteenth, the Sun King? Became king of France at the age of *four,* ruled for seventy-two years, longer than any other ruler in European history? Or the Dalai Lama? Formally recognized as the spiritual leader of Tibetan Buddhists and the monarch of Tibet at the age of *four*? Well, I'm a lot older than four, sweetie, and I'm a lot smarter than that fat slob we've got for an Ont Queen now."

This is dangerous talk, Cheyenne thought. *If somebody heard her talking this way, she could get into terrible trouble. Would she take such a chance if she wasn't serious? Maybe she* is *serious.*

Betsy stuck her head out the door and

looked down the hallway, then came back into the classroom.

"Hedy will return any minute now," said Betsy, "so I'd better wrap this up. You might be interested to know that all the mutants are behind me on this. We aren't out to kill humans like the onts are—we're part human ourselves, you know. We want to be separate from humans, but equal. If you're willing to work with us, you'll be helping to defeat the onts. What do you say?"

Do I dare to answer her? Cheyenne wondered. *What if it* is *a trick?*

"Tell you what," said Betsy. "To prove this isn't a trick, if you agree to work with us, I'll sneak you into the garage where they put the buses so you can take pictures with that little digital camera you've got in your pocket."

How the heck does she know about the camera?

"Do you want to take pictures of the buses or not?" Betsy asked.

"Okay," said Cheyenne.

The buses, six of them, stood in the gloom of the underground garage. As Betsy kept watch, Cheyenne took out her digital camera and squeezed off a few shots. The camera flashed briefly in the darkened cavern.

"What did they do with all the people who were on the buses?" Cheyenne whispered.

"Hypnotized them and put them to work, I guess," said Betsy.

"Doing what?"

"I don't know," said Betsy. "Taking care of the babies, working with the aphids in the dairy, stuff like that. You done yet, idiot? I really don't want anyone to catch us in here."

"Can you take me to see some of them?" Cheyenne asked.

"It's pretty risky."

"You don't seem to mind taking risks," said Cheyenne.

"Okay," said Betsy.

Before they even entered, they heard the sounds of the heavy machinery—THRUM . . . POCK!

THRUM . . . POCK! THRUM . . . POCK! went the Snot Presses. TA-POCKETA-POCKETA-QUEEP! TA-POCKETA-POCKETA-QUEEP! TA-POCKETA-POCKETA-QUEEP! went the Odor Extractors.

Cheyenne marveled at how much space the snot processing plant occupied. The small Snot Press and Odor Extractor machines she and Wally had seen in the cellar of Mandible House were multiplied a thousand times in the underground factory, which stretched the length of a football field. Clear glass tubing as big around as adult anacondas was filled with grayish-green hot snot, bubbling and surging overhead, then branching out into many narrower capillaries before plunging into vast tubs.

"Where did they get all that snot?" Cheyenne whispered.

"You should know, sweetie," said Betsy. "From what I hear, you and the Mandible sisters started the entire flu epidemic in Cincinnati."

Attending the machinery were an army of humans, moving like zombies and wearing bright yellow jumpsuits with the huge purple letters QOUF stenciled on their backs.

Cheyenne slipped her digital camera out of her jeans pocket and took a few pictures.

"What does Q-O-U-F stand for?" Cheyenne whispered.

"Queen Ont Underground Facility," whispered Betsy in an annoyed voice. "I knew you're ugly. They didn't warn me you're also stupid."

"If you really think I'm stupid, you wouldn't have recruited me to help you get rid of the

queen," whispered Cheyenne. "And why don't we check out who's really stupid here. Let's see now. Am I the one who thinks she can overthrow an entire army of onts with just a few mutant kids? Oh no, wait, that's *you*. And while we're at it, look who's calling who *ugly*."

"I'm rubber, you're glue," whispered Betsy. "Everything you say bounces off me and sticks to you."

"Turd face!" whispered Cheyenne.

"Fart blossom!" whispered Betsy.

They stuck out their tongues at each other, put their thumbs in their ears, and waggled their fingers.

CHAPTER 15

Eating Children: A Matter of Conscience?

(From the *Ghouls Gazette,* a private newsletter)

Eatin' Good in the Neighborhood

By Wolfgang Stumpf

If there's one thing we ghouls adore, it's kids. Big kids, little kids, boy kids, girl kids—they're all delicious. Simmered in a stew with baby carrots, new potatoes, and little pearl onions or simply slathered with mustard and stuffed in a bun, children of every sort are a naughty treat.

I can just see you squeamish ghouls crinkling up your noses and saying *Eeoooow.* I suppose you wouldn't *dream* of skulking through Dripping Fang Forest at night, plucking a kid out of a pup tent, and popping him or her into a skillet for dinner. I suppose you think that strolling into a Piggly Wiggly market and buying the little darlings already frozen in TV dinners—surrounded by green peas and junior fries in a little aluminum tray, with no noses, toes, or tiny fingers to remind you of their previous state—is somehow more civilized.

Well, it's not. Buying them frozen is no better than trapping them live. Doesn't matter if you're the one who did the actual plucking or not. It's the same argument humans use who protest the wearing of fur coats: Remove one from the store, and somewhere, somebody is going to have to remove one from the population to take its place.

I won't pretend that eating children doesn't trouble me at all. I am not a monster. I prefer not to learn their little names or what their little hobbies are, or to see the little stuffed toys they sleep with at night. Once, just before cooking her, my wife and I had the misfortune of seeing the child we had chosen, clutching her little stuffed teddy bear. That ruined the whole experience for me. I had to let the child go. We dined that night on *moo shu* chicken from the local Chinese take-out place.

So, the eating of children has always come with problems. Now we have something new to worry about.

Ghoul medical research has just come up with a real shocker: The eating of children was found to be the number one cause of premature heart attacks among ghouls. Ghouls who eat children live less than 250 years!

This news has rocked the ghoul population. We have always suspected there might be some connection between the eating of children and heart attacks, but nobody has attempted to prove it before. Well, I, for one, refuse to believe the research. I have always dined on children, and I'm certainly not going to stop now just because some overzealous ghouls in long white coats did some probably poorly conceived experiments. If you believe them, you might as well believe human medical researchers who say that smoking causes cancer!

So what will it be tonight—breaded child cutlets? Boys in boysenberry sauce? Grilled girl? Filet *de fille*? French-fried fingers? Steak-and-kiddie pie? I can't wait to go home tonight and find out what my cunning little wife has prepared for us! *Bon appétit!*

CHAPTER 16

You May Be On to Something Very Big

"May I help you?" asked the FBI receptionist. It wasn't the same receptionist as the last time. This one had coarser hair and wrinklier skin.

"Yes," said Wally. "We're Wally and Cheyenne Shluffmuffin. We were here the other day to see Special Agent Cromwell. We need to see him again."

"Do you have an appointment?"

"No," said Wally.

"And what was this in reference to?" asked the receptionist.

"We have some photographs he might think are interesting," said Cheyenne.

"One moment please."

The receptionist buzzed somebody on her intercom. "Sir," she said, "I have two children out here at the desk, Wally and Cheyenne . . ." She looked at the twins questioningly.

"Shluffmuffin," said Cheyenne.

"Wally and Cheyenne Shluffmuffin. They claim to have some photographs you might think are interesting. Yes, sir. I'll send them right in." She turned to the twins. "Room two-oh-five-nine, down the hall."

"Thank you," said Cheyenne.

Cheyenne and Wally walked down the familiar long hallway to room 2059.

Special Agent Cromwell was still sitting behind his desk, eating pistachio nuts from a silver bowl. He even had on the same suit and tie as when they'd seen him the last time. It was possible he had never left.

"Nice to see you again," said Cromwell. "I hear you've got some photographs to show me."

Cheyenne nodded and held out a large brown envelope.

"Are these going to convince me the passengers on the six missing buses were kidnapped by giant ants?" he asked with a smile.

"I don't know what would convince you of that, sir," said Cheyenne. "You'd have to look at the pictures and make up your own mind."

Cromwell took the envelope and shook the photos out on the desk. He picked them up one by one and studied them, pursing his lips and extending them outward. He looked like a fish.

"Where did you say these were taken?" he asked.

"We didn't say," said Cheyenne. "But they were taken in the underground garage and the snot processing plant of the Ont Queen's cave."

Cromwell nodded, studying the pictures some more. "What are those machines they're operating?" he asked.

"Snot Presses and Odor Extractors, sir," said Cheyenne.

"And these people in the yellow jumpsuits," he said. "These are the people who were on the buses?"

"Right," said Cheyenne.

"Who took these pictures?"

"I did," said Cheyenne.

"Why did the giant ants allow you to take these pictures?" he asked.

"They didn't," said Cheyenne.

"Then how did you get in there?"

"It's a little complicated."

"Tell me anyway," said Cromwell.

"Okay," said Cheyenne. "The Ont Queen sent for me to come to the cave to train the mutant ont kids to control humans. They thought I was under posthypnotic suggestion, but I wasn't, because my brother had snapped me out of it before I left the house. One of the mutant kids who wants to start a revolution to overthrow the queen thinks I can help her, so she snuck me into the garage and the snot processing plant as a favor."

Cromwell stared at her for so long, she wondered if he'd heard her.

"Sir, did you hear what I said?" she asked.

Cromwell nodded. "All right, here's what I'm going to do," he said finally. "I'm probably going to lose my job over this, but I have a gut feeling you're not putting me on here. I'll have these photos checked out by our people. I'll have them computer enhanced and analyzed and compared to the photos of the folks who were kidnapped. If they're who you say they are . . . Well, I think you two may be on to something very big here."

Cheyenne and Wally beamed.

"If these photos check out," Cromwell continued, "I'm going to personally helicopter you guys out to Quantico, our FBI training facility in Virginia. Together we'll brief top management and our SWAT team. Then the SWAT team will be sent to Dripping Fang Forest to penetrate the Ont Queen's cave so we can extract the prisoners and arrest those giant ants. How does that sound to you?"

"It sounds great, sir," said Cheyenne.

"It sounds okay, sir," said Wally.

"You're a very brave girl to do what you've done, Cheyenne," said Cromwell. "And you two kids have performed a very great service to your city, your state, and your country."

"Thank you, sir," said Cheyenne proudly.

"Thank you, sir," said Wally.

Cromwell stood and shook hands with each of them. "I'll call you as soon as my people have analyzed the photos," he said.

As soon as the twins got out of Cromwell's office, they gave each other high fives.

"Shluffmuffins rule!" said Cheyenne.

"We're going to Quantico on an FBI chopper!" said Wally.

They walked past the receptionist's desk.

"So long," said Cheyenne.

"Good afternoon, children," said the receptionist.

The intercom on her desk buzzed. The receptionist picked up the phone. "Yes, sir?" she said. "Very well, sir. I'll be right in."

She left the desk and walked down the long hallway to room 2059.

Cromwell looked up from Cheyenne's photographs.

"Miss Crawford," said Cromwell, "please take these photographs over to Photo Analysis and ask

Special Agent Morrison to try to match them to shots we have of the kidnapped people on the buses."

"Where were these photographs taken, sir?" asked the receptionist.

"In Dripping Fang Forest," said Cromwell. "In some underground cave, I believe. The children seem to feel it's populated by giant ants ruled by somebody called the Ont Queen. They claim the onts are plotting to enslave mankind and end life on Earth as we know it."

The receptionist smiled, then picked up a couple of pictures and looked at them. "And you believe them?" she asked. "You believe an army of giant ants is plotting to enslave human beings?"

"I know it sounds crazy," said Cromwell, "but yeah, I kind of do."

She nodded. "Do you happen to have the time, sir?"

"The time? Oh, sure." Cromwell raised his left wrist and glanced at his watch. "It's a little after three. Three-thirteen, to be precise."

"Really?" she said. "It can't be after three already. May I see that?"

She took his hand and held it briefly, but instead of looking at his watch she pressed her ring against the inside of his wrist.

Cromwell seemed surprised, as if momentarily pained. Then his expression froze, and he slumped forward on his desk, his head falling facedown into the silver bowl of pistachio nuts.

The receptionist placed her fingertips on Cromwell's neck near his Adam's apple, against his carotid artery. Then she picked up the photographs and took them over to the electric shredder. She turned it on and fed the photographs into the shredder, one by one. Then she turned off the machine, picked up the phone on Cromwell's desk, and dialed a number within the building.

"This is an emergency," she said into the phone. "Special Agent Cromwell in room 2059 has just suffered a massive heart attack. I need immediate medical assistance."

Then the receptionist got an outside line and dialed a number in the city. "This is an emergency," she said into the phone. "The Shluffmuffin twins, Walter and Cheyenne, are leaving the building. They know too much. They need to be terminated as quickly as possible."

She hung up the phone and adjusted something under her chin, which was wrinklier than before. Part of her rubber mask had developed a little too much slack.

CHAPTER 17

There Seems to Be a Slight Problem with Your Credit Report

"So, Mr. Shluffmuffin," said a voice. "We meet again. I told you I'd be back, and now here I am, just as I promised."

Dad turned around to see the troll from the pawnshop had again entered the house unnoticed. And this time he'd brought a friend, another troll. The new troll had lots more warts on his face, and all of them sprouted hairs. Small curved tusks grew out of both sides of his face.

"This is my associate, Mr. Terwilliger," said the first troll.

"How did you get in here?" Dad asked.

"How we got in is not important," said the

first troll. "The important thing is that we are here now. The even more important thing is that you have broken your sacred word, Mr. Shluffmuffin. You have failed to pay us the interest on your loan, and now we have come to collect the full amount that is due us."

"I really feel terrible about what I owe you," said Dad.

"I believe you, Mr. Shluffmuffin," said the troll. "I believe you feel terrible. I also believe that soon you will feel even more terrible. In fact, how you feel now is giddy with joy compared to how you will soon be feeling."

"I've been scrambling to earn the money to pay you," said Dad, "and I've raised almost all of it, but the thing is—"

The troll held up both his palms.

"Please, Mr. Shluffmuffin," he said. "Do not insult my intelligence. No more excuses." He turned to the other troll. "Mr. Terwilliger?"

Both trolls came toward Dad. The one called Mr. Terwilliger got him in a headlock. The other one punched him in the stomach.

"Oof!" cried Dad. "Now just wait a minute!"

"No, Mr. Shluffmuffin, we are through waiting."

"I really wish you hadn't done that," said Dad.

"Really? Then you're also going to wish we hadn't done *this,*" said the troll, kicking Dad in the shins and stomping on both of his feet.

"Ouch!" said Dad. "Okay, I'm starting to get mad now."

"Oooo, he's starting to get *mad* now," mimicked the troll. "I'm terrified, aren't you, Mr. Terwilliger?"

Just then Edgar Spydelle walked into the house. "I say!" he exclaimed. "What the bloody devil is going on in here?"

"Nothing to worry about, Edgar," said Dad. "These gentlemen have just come to collect some money I borrowed from them, but they'll be leaving now."

The first troll pulled out a heavy automatic pistol.

Edgar hurriedly left the room.

"All right, that's it," said Dad. "Weapons are

where I draw the line. Weapons are definitely *not* allowed in this house."

Both trolls erupted in laughter. Dad ran at the troll who held the gun. The gun went off with an unexpectedly loud door-slam explosion, and a bullet tore through Dad's chest.

But Dad kept running, and with one hand he picked the troll up by his long floppy ears.

"Oww! Hey!" cried the troll.

Dad bared his fangs and spread his leathery wings.

Both trolls' eyes nearly popped out of their sockets.

"I g-give up," gasped the troll who was hanging by his ears. "Please don't hurt me!"

"Do you like baseball?" Dad asked.

"W-what?" said the troll.

"I said, do you like baseball?"

"Y-y-yes. Why?"

"Let's play ball," said Dad. "Batter up!"

Dad tossed the first troll high in the air, grabbed the second troll around the ankles, and swung him like a bat, smacking the first troll clear

across the room. "Base hit!" Dad yelled. "Man on first!"

The trolls picked themselves painfully off the floor.

"Okay, Mr. Shluffmuffin," said the first troll, "forget the money. We're even!"

Both trolls limped toward the front door. Dad grabbed them by the ears.

"Not so fast," said Dad. "A deal's a deal." He reached into his pocket and counted out a number of bills. "Here's the money I borrowed," he said, stuffing the bills into the first troll's pocket. "Sadly, though, I can't pay you your outrageous rate of interest."

"Hey," said the first troll, "no problem, Mr. Shluffmuffin. It turns out that was an interest-free loan. Glad to be of service."

"Thank you," said Dad, extending his hand. "I appreciate it. But, one more thing before you go."

The troll reached into his pocket and, with trembling fingers, gave back Dad's driver's license.

"Don't mess with the dead," said Dad.

CHAPTER 18

A Fatal Sneeze

Cheyenne and Wally made their way slowly up the forest path to the Spydelles' house, blissfully unaware that they were being watched and followed. They stopped in front of the house and paused while they took out their keys.

Twenty feet above them, a shadowy figure dressed in camouflage hunter's clothing was hiding in the trees. It was The Jackal, the internationally famous assassin who'd been hired by the Ont Queen to kill Wally but who'd failed miserably on two previous attempts.

The Jackal took a dart out of his pocket. The dart had an inch-long steel point, the tip of which had been dipped in poison made from a poison dart frog.

The poison dart frog is the deadliest creature in the world, with enough poison in it to kill ten humans. These tiny tree frogs are about an inch and a half long and come in exquisite colors and patterns—bright yellow, electric blue, or red and gold striped. Indian tribes catch them and put them near a fire. When the frogs grow hot, their skin produces a slime, which the Indians scrape off and make into a potent poison into which they dip the tips of their darts and arrows.

The Jackal placed the dart into his four-foot-long bamboo blowgun and raised the gun to his lips. Just then a warm wind carried pollen from a nearby ragweed plant past his nose and made it itch.

"I'm pumped that we're going to be helicoptered to Quantico!" said Cheyenne. "It will be so cool to meet with the SWAT teams and tell them how to free the prisoners and arrest everybody in the ant cave. Hey, do you think they'd let us help them?"

"Is that a serious question?" asked Wally. "Are you really asking if I think the FBI is going to let civilians—civilian *kids*—be part of a SWAT-team military action?"

"Well, maybe you're right," said Cheyenne. "Still, it would be so cool."

Ten feet to the side of the Spydelles' doorway, behind a large boulder, crouched two massive figures dressed in black—the Stumpfs. They wore masks and carried small glass bottles of chloroform. Each of them opened a bottle and poured a few drops of chloroform into a tissue.

"Boy," said Cheyenne, "I hope the SWAT team doesn't have to kill any of my friends."

"Any of your *friends*?" said Wally. "What friends do you have in the ont cave?"

"Well, you know," said Cheyenne a little sheepishly. "Hedy and, uh, Betsy and stuff."

"Betsy?" said Wally. "Betsy, the mutant ont kid who says she hates you? Betsy, who bit you so hard it bled? *That* Betsy is your friend?"

"Well, maybe she wasn't *then,*" said Cheyenne, "but maybe she is *now.* I mean, we were getting along pretty well when I left the ont cave with the photographs."

Wally shook his head in disgust. "I don't believe you," he said.

"What don't you believe?" Cheyenne asked.

"How you can be so . . . so . . ."

". . . friendly?" said Cheyenne. "I happen to be a friendly person, Wally. I happen to like people, okay? Not like *some* people I could name."

"You don't think I'm friendly?" asked Wally. "You don't think I like people?"

"Not all that much," said Cheyenne.

"Ready, Sweet Lips?" whispered Mrs. Stumpf.

"On my signal, Piggy Toes," whispered Mr. Stumpf.

The Jackal steadied his blowgun on a branch, sighted it on Cheyenne's neck, and took a deep breath. His nose really tickled inside, but he stifled a sneeze.

"Now!" whispered Mr. Stumpf.

The Stumpfs waddled out from behind the boulder.

"Huh?" said Cheyenne, startled at the

Stumpfs' sudden appearance, staggering backward.

The hunter blew.

The dart flew.

And it split the air precisely where Cheyenne's neck had been a half second earlier and embedded itself deep in the Spydelles' front door.

"Cheyenne, look out!" yelled Wally. He pushed her to the ground and fell on top of

her. "Somebody in that tree up there is trying to kill us!"

The Jackal cursed under his breath, wiped his now-runny nose, and hurried to place another dart in his blowgun.

Wally picked up a rock and threw it at The Jackal. Because he was throwing from a prone position on top of Cheyenne, the rock missed its mark—but it got The Jackal so rattled, he put his second dart in the blowgun backward.

Meanwhile, the Stumpfs lumbered up to the twins, chloroformed tissues in hand.

The Jackal raised the blowgun to his lips. Again the ragweed pollen tickled the inside of

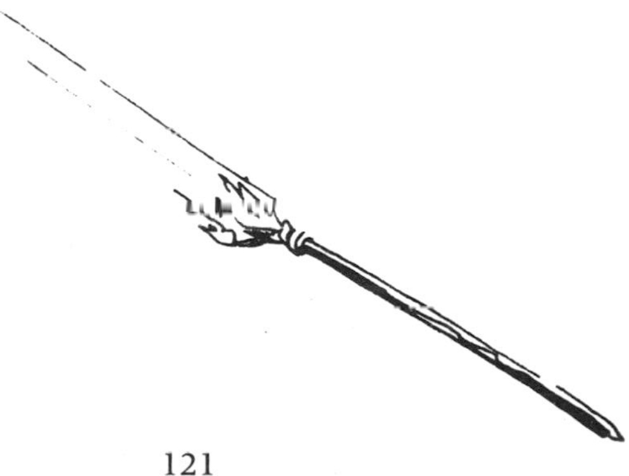

his nose. He sighted the blowgun on the back of Wally's neck and tried to fight off a tremendous sneeze: "Ah . . . ah . . . AH . . ." But no CHOO! ever followed, because the intake of air on the third *AH* had sucked the dart into The Jackal's throat, paralyzing him instantly. The Jackal's eyes glazed over, and he dropped out of the tree, dead before he hit the ground.

Mrs. Stumpf screamed as the body hit the dirt.

Wally and Cheyenne, who might otherwise have been able to fight off the slow-moving Stumpfs, were so startled by The Jackal's body dropping out of the tree, they didn't get out of the Stumpfs' way in time. The Stumps fell on top of them, the chloroformed tissues finding their marks. A moment later, both twins were unconscious.

"It worked, Lamb Pie, it worked!" said Mr. Stumpf.

"Now comes the fun part, Turtledove!" said Mrs. Stumpf.

Mr. Stumpf threw Wally's unconscious body over his shoulder.

Mrs. Stumpf threw Cheyenne's over hers.

And then, hand in hand, they lumbered out of the Spydelles' yard and off in the direction of home and the best dinner of the month.

"Oh, my word!" said Edgar, as he entered his front yard and caught sight of the dead body on the ground. "*There's* a pity."

He felt for a pulse and found none.

"Shirley!" he called. "Might I see you out here a moment, my dear? I fear somebody has expired on our doorstep."

A moment later the door opened, and Shirley appeared.

"Oh, what a shame!" she said. "Is he . . . ?"

"Dead as a mackerel, I'm afraid," said Edgar. "Poor chap. I wonder how it happened."

Edgar rolled the body over, studied its glazed eyes and open mouth. He reached into the mouth and removed the dart.

"Well, I'm not a forensics expert," said Edgar, "but I daresay this dart had something to do with the poor devil's demise. Wonder what he was doing swallowing a dart. I say, are the twins about?"

"Not yet," said Shirley, "but I expect them home shortly. They went to the FBI with those pictures today, you know. I can't wait to hear how *that* went."

CHAPTER 19

Waiter, There's an Orphan in My Soup

The Stumpfs' home was simple but comfy. There were oversized couches with overstuffed pillows to cushion their massive buttocks. Soft carpets to deaden the trudge of their heavy feet.

The kitchen was the largest room in the house. It had a long counter and two freestanding tiled islands with deep stainless-steel sinks, and it looked more like a morgue than a kitchen. The stove was larger than those of most restaurants. On the stove now was a tremendous kettle filled with water. All the burners were on underneath it, burning hot and blue. There was a faint smell of gas from the burners.

Mr. and Mrs. Stumpf carried the unconscious Shluffmuffin children into the kitchen. Mr. Stumpf put Wally down on one of the tiled islands, and Mrs. Stumpf put Cheyenne down on the other.

"Don't they look lovely when they sleep?" asked Mrs. Stumpf.

"Delicious," said Mr. Stumpf, "absolutely delicious. Well, let's get to work. I'm so hungry, my stomach thinks my throat's cut."

Mrs. Stumpf chuckled. "Why don't you get the vegetables ready, Kitten Face, while I clean up the kids?" she said.

"Good idea, Bunny Ears," said Mr. Stumpf.

Mrs. Stumpf took off Wally's muddy sneakers and socks and dropped them into a big garbage bag. She wrinkled her nose at the acrid barn-animal smell.

Humming a happy tune from a production of *The Phantom of the Opera* that they'd seen in Cincinnati only a week before, Mrs. Stumpf peeled the dirty clothes off both Wally and Cheyenne and, wrinkling her nose with distaste, dropped the clothes into the garbage bag. Then, with a soft pink washcloth dipped in Joy, she lovingly washed and scrubbed both children as if she were giving them their evening baths.

When she was finished, they were sweet smelling and spotless. She kissed their foreheads and wrapped them tightly in cheesecloth sacks up to their necks. Then both she and Mr. Stumpf put tarragon, thyme, celery, sage, basil, oregano, black peppercorns, sliced onions, and cloves of garlic into the cheesecloth sacks with them.

Wally groaned.

"Uh-oh," said Mrs. Stumpf, "they're beginning to wake, Love Bug. We'd better hurry."

Each Stumpf grabbed a seasoned child-cheesecloth sack, carried it over to the big kettle on the stove, and gently seated it in the warm bathtubby water.

"Make sure they don't slump over now," chided Mrs. Stumpf as she threw a load of fingerling potatoes into the water. "It wouldn't do to have them drown before they boil, you know. Drowning tends to spoil the flavor a bit."

"You can say *that* again," said Mr. Stumpf, chuckling at a memory best forgotten.

Then she carefully fitted a huge stainless-steel pot cover with two holes in the middle over the children's heads and locked it down.

Cheyenne was having a delicious dream. She was in an outdoor hot tub in a hotel on a Caribbean island. The sun was baking her skin in a pleasant way, and she was glad she'd slathered on plenty of sunblock. A palm tree with large drooping fronds swayed gently in the breeze. Cheyenne could hear the sound of the waves crashing on the nearby beach—the rumbling-grumbling-tumbledown roar and hiss. And from somewhere came the fragrant spices of whatever outrageous and tempting delicacy the hotel chef was cooking up for lunch on his little outdoor grill.

Wally was the first to wake up.

"Wh-where am I?" he asked. He looked around. He realized he couldn't move. "Hey, what is this? What's going on here?"

"Well, good evening, Mr. Sleepyhead," said Mrs. Stumpf. "Did you have a nice nap?"

That's when Cheyenne woke up.

"What's happening?" she asked. "Wally, where are we?"

"I don't know," he said. "But this is the creepy couple who wanted to adopt us, the Stumpfs. What are you doing to us?" he asked them.

"Why, isn't it obvious, dear?" said Mrs. Stumpf. "We're having you for dinner."

"Is this some kind of a joke?" said Wally.

"Why, no," said Mrs. Stumpf. "Does it *seem* like a joke?"

"Let us out of here this minute!" Wally demanded. "This water is getting really hot!"

"Oh, simmer down," said Mr. Stumpf.

"What are we supposed to do," said Wally, "promise you money to let us out?"

"No, dear, you're supposed to *cook,*" said Mrs. Stumpf.

"How long are you planning to leave us in this pot?" Cheyenne demanded.

"Until you're done, dear," said Mrs. Stumpf. She turned to her husband. "You know, Mouse Breath, maybe we ought to leave them alone now till they're cooked. I never enjoy this part. It's the same with lobsters. I just feel their pain too much."

"You're so tenderhearted, Puppy Whiskers," said Mr. Stumpf.

"I just can't stand seeing the poor things suffer," said Mrs. Stumpf.

"How long before they're done?" asked Mr. Stumpf.

"About forty minutes should be enough," said Mrs. Stumpf.

"Why don't we go to the bakery and pick up a nice key lime mousse and chocolate peanut-butter pie?" said Mr. Stumpf. "By the time we get back, they'll be cooked and ready to carve, and we can skip all the yelling and screaming."

"What a lovely idea," said Mrs. Stumpf. "I do so prefer to skip the yelling and screaming. Well, see you later, children. Don't be sad, it will all be over very soon, and you will be delicious."

The water was now about as hot as the water in a Jacuzzi. It wasn't really unpleasant yet, but in a short time it would be boiling and the pain would be too intense for the twins to even think.

"This is the worst thing that's ever happened to us," said Wally.

"Oh, I don't know," said Cheyenne. "We've been through *lots* of tough times, Wally. Remember when the Mandible sisters first adopted us and found out we knew they were breeding a race of super-ants? They locked us in our rooms and told us they were going to kill us in the morning."

"Yeah, that was pretty bad."

"Or the time we were lost in the swamp and starving to death, and we had to eat centipedes and caterpillars to stay alive?" asked Cheyenne. "Or the time you were drowning in the aquarium tank with that giant octopus and it was about to eat you?"

"Yeah, both of those were pretty bad, too," said Wally.

"We've been in lots of tough situations," said Cheyenne, "but you always figure out some way to get us out of them. I know you will this time, too."

"Cheyenne, we are stuck in a pot of *boiling water,*" said Wally. "We're going to *scald to death* in a few minutes, and two ghouls are going to *eat us for dinner.* How am I going to get us out of this?"

"I don't know, Wally, but you always do," said Cheyenne. "Besides, it could be worse."

"How could it possibly be worse than this?" Wally asked.

"We could get out of this pot, and you could see me naked," said Cheyenne.

Wally rolled his eyes and sighed. Sometimes Cheyenne could be impossible. Not that he wanted her to see *him* naked, but that wouldn't be worse than being boiled to death by two humongous ghouls. As bad, maybe, but not worse.

"You know what?" said Cheyenne. "I just tore a hole in this cheesecloth bag. I think I could get completely out of it if I tried."

"Really?" Wally said. "Then how are we supposed to get out of this pot, genius? It's locked shut."

"How about rocking back and forth till it tips over?" said Cheyenne. "Maybe the top will break off or something."

"Rocking back and forth till it tips *over*?" said Wally disgustedly. "Cheyenne that's absolutely . . . You know what? That's actually not such a terrible idea. Let's try it."

They started rocking the pot from side to side. The hot water and potatoes sloshed back and forth. Pretty soon they got a good rhythm going, back and forth, back and forth. The pot tipped further and further on each rock. Finally, it tipped over completely and fell to the floor with a loud *CLANG!* The top popped off.

The force of hitting the ground slammed them into the pot and almost knocked them unconscious. For a moment the twins lay on the kitchen floor in a huge puddle of hot water and wet potatoes as tiny points of light circled in front of their eyes. Then the tiny points of light faded and disappeared.

"We did it!" shouted Wally.

"I told you you'd get us out of this!" said Cheyenne.

"It was *your* idea," said Wally. "You were the one who saved us this time."

They tried to stand.

"Don't you *dare* look at me, Wally Shluffmuffin!" shrieked Cheyenne, trying to cover all her private parts at once with her hands and arms.

"Don't look at *me*!" shouted Wally, bent over, clutching his crotch, folded up like a collapsed umbrella.

Still hunched over in grotesque postures in vain attempts to hide their secret areas, Wally and Cheyenne ran through the house, searching for clothing. They found some belonging to Mr. and Mrs. Stumpf, but the clothes fit them like pup

tents. Eventually, they found their own clothes jammed into a garbage bag. Sitting on the floor with their backs to each other, they got dressed.

"It's been at least a half hour since those ghouls left for the bakery," said Wally. "We'd better get out of here fast before they come back."

Wally looked around the kitchen—at the giant kettle lying on the floor, at the puddles of water and the potatoes. "We probably have at least five minutes before they get back," he said. "It's a shame to leave them with nothing for dinner. And I do hate to leave a messy house."

Cheyenne smiled.

"I think we can fix that," she said.

Together they lifted the kettle back onto the stove, put all the potatoes back inside it, and mopped up the water.

"Are potatoes really enough, or should we give them something a little more substantial?" asked Wally.

They looked around the house for things to put into the kettle. They added a quart of maple syrup, a dozen eggs with crushed shells, some old sponges, two pairs of huge tennis shoes, a gallon of floor wax, three rolls of toilet paper, and a gigantic pair of Mrs. Stumpf's pink underpants. They put the cover back on the kettle, locked it in place, and turned the burners on high.

"Now at least they'll have some nourishing stew to go with that pie," said Cheyenne.

They turned on all the faucets in the house, and giggling hysterically, they slipped out the back door.

"I've got to tell you something," said Wally, once they were back in the leafy forest and on the way to the Spydelles'.

"What?"

"When we were dressing back there?" said Wally. "I saw your butt."

Cheyenne punched her brother on the arm.

"I saw yours, too," she said. "I saw *everything.*"

They giggled and punched each other on the arms and shoulders until they were black and blue.

What's Next for the Shluffmuffin Twins?

Wow, Cheyenne and Wally almost didn't make it that time. If Cheyenne hadn't thought to rock the kettle, the twins would have literally ended up in the soup. Too bad we couldn't wait and see the ghouls discover what the twins left in the kettle instead. How steamed must the ghouls have been to learn the twins *weren't*.

Wonder what'll happen when the onts begin their nefarious scheme to plant mutant children in human families and destroy them from within. Wonder who'll be unlucky enough to adopt a mutant as unpleasant as Betsy.

Wonder what'll happen when Hedy Mandible and the Ont Queen find The Jackal not only failed to kill Wally again but terminated himself as well. They may not stop trying to kill Wally, but who'll they find to do the job? And by what horrid means? There can't be anything worse than what poor Wally's already had to escape—like that four-hundred-pound octopus in Book Six.

Maybe it'll be a killer with a machete, a garrote, or a chain saw. Maybe somebody will suspend a heavy safe in the air with a rope, trick Wally into walking underneath it, then cut the rope. Maybe somebody will capture him, take him to a sawmill, and chain him to a platform, which brings him closer and closer to the teeth of a whining saw blade. Maybe somebody will tie him to a railroad track in the path of a speeding train—the engineer won't see him till it's too late, and he'll try in vain to brake the thundering engine as it hurtles down the slick steel rails toward the hapless boy. How hideous a death *that* would be.

Well, at least it would be *fast*. Much better than, say, being attacked by poisonous snakes. Hey, could there be a worse way to die than finding a twelve-foot-long king cobra or a black mamba slithering toward you on its belly, its forked tongue flicking in and out, its hollow fangs ready to inject a poison that'll shut down your nervous system, paralyze your limbs and lungs, and make it impossible for you to draw another breath? Whew! Lucky the poor twins won't have to deal with anything as hideous as *that.*

Wait a minute. We've just been handed the title of Secrets of Dripping Fang, Book Eight, and it's . . . Oh no. Oh *no*! This is too ghastly for words! The title of Book Eight is . . . *When Bad Snakes Attack Good Children.*

Dan Greenburg writes the popular Zack Files series for kids and has also written many bestselling books for grown-ups. His seventy books have been translated into twenty languages. To research his writing, Dan has worked with N.Y. firefighters and homicide cops, searched for the Loch Ness monster, flown upside down in an open-cockpit plane, taken part in voodoo ceremonies in Haiti, and disciplined tigers on a Texas ranch. He has not, however, personally encountered any giant octopuses or ghouls—at least not yet. Dan lives north of New York with wife Judith, son Zack, and many cats.

Scott M. Fischer glided through high school doing extra-credit art assignments for math teachers, which is kinda boring stuff to draw. Next he went to art school, where he learned to paint even more boring things—like flower vases. However, he swears that since then he has drawn nothing but cool stuff—like oozy, drooling monsters, treacherous villains, and the occasional flower vase that has fangs and eats flowers for breakfast!